The Monsters

Reggie grinned. "Kate, you're staying with Wanda Barnes for the week, right? Keep your eye on her brother Will — he's *something*."

"Oh, great!" Kate groaned.

"Of course, the twins aren't exactly relaxing either," Reggie went on. "And then there's Frank — the best wrestler at Walden High."

"Sounds perfect," said Kate. "I'm spending a week with three monsters and the Incredible Hulk."

Look for these and other books in the Sleepover
Friends Series:

Kate's Sleepover Disaster

Susan Saunders

AN
APPLE
PAPERBACK

SCHOLASTIC INC.
New York Toronto London Auckland Sydney

ISBN 0-590-41846-7

12 11 10 9 8 7 6 5 4 3 2 1   9/8 0 1 2 3 4/9

Printed in the U.S.A.   28

First Scholastic printing, May 1989

Chapter
1

"What do you think of this black-and-white sweatshirt with my red stretchpants?" Stephanie Green asked. She slipped the sweatshirt on over a long-sleeved T-shirt. Then she pulled the red stretchpants out of her bedroom closet and held them up to her waist.

Kate Beekman was sitting at Stephanie's desk, making a list of things she planned to pack for our week in Walden. She glanced up just long enough to shake her head. "It'd be okay for going shopping — but for a day on a farm?"

Stephanie smiled at herself in the full-length mirror on the closet door. "Not everybody in Walden lives on a farm. Besides, *I* like it!" she murmured. "What about you, Patti?"

1

Patti Jenkins was sitting on the floor, playing with Stephanie's kitten, Cinders. "You look great in those colors," Patti replied in her soft voice.

Stephanie has pink cheeks and dark, curly hair, so she does look good in red, black, and white. Which is just as well, because she hardly ever wears anything else. Even her bedroom is red, black, and white!

Stephanie turned to face me — I'm Lauren Hunter — as I was stretched out on one of the beds, reading an old issue of *Teen* magazine. "Lauren? The red stretchpants or black sweats?"

"I can't make important decisions while my stomach is yelling for food," I said. "Are there any cookies left?" Stephanie's mother makes fantastic peanut-butter chocolate-chip cookies.

"Another whole plateful." Stephanie pointed to her chest-of-drawers, where she'd set the plate to keep it out of Cinders' way. "You really are depressing, Lauren," she added with a sigh. "I don't understand how you can eat so much and never gain an ounce. I barely *look* at a cookie, and I blow up like a balloon!" Stephanie puffed out her cheeks and frowned at the mirror.

"You do not," I said, putting down *Teen* and sitting up. "Our faces are different shapes, that's all."

My face is long and thin — in fact, I'm long and thin in general. Stephanie's face is kind of roundish. "But if you're worried about gaining weight, you ought to exercise."

Stephanie shook her head. "Jogging three times a week, like you do with your brother? No way — sweating makes my hair frizzy." She folded up the red stretchpants and crammed them into a large suitcase on the second bed. "I don't care what you say, Kate — I'm taking these. I don't necessarily have to wear them to milk cows."

"Or parade around in front of any bulls, either, I hope," Kate teased. "You know what red does to *them*."

It was late Wednesday afternoon, after school. Kate, Stephanie, Patti, and I spend most of our free after-school time together. We're together during school, too, because all of us are in 5B, Mrs. Mead's class, at Riverhurst Elementary. A bunch of the kids in our class were going upstate to stay with some fifth-graders in Walden, a farming town. It was kind of an exchange program our teachers had cooked up — Mrs. Mead is friends with Ms. Powell, a fifth grade teacher in Walden. First the Walden kids had visited us in Riverhurst, and now it was our turn to visit them.

"I hate to pack," I said, snaring a handful of cookies. "I've changed my mind about what to take so many times already that I'll probably end up with six pairs of jeans and no sweaters, or leave all my socks at home, or something dumb like that."

"You should try packing with Melissa the Monster around," Kate said from the desk. Melissa is Kate's seven-year-old sister, and she can be a real pill. "Last night I was pretty close to a final decision about my clothes for the trip. I'd piled the stuff I was planning to take on one end of my bed, and everything I'd rejected on the other end. I went into the bathroom to wash my hair. When I came back out, both piles of clothes were totally messed up — and Melissa was waltzing up and down the stairs in my new blue stretchpants! I wanted to kill her!"

"I think you're too hard on Melissa," said Stephanie to Kate's reflection in the mirror.

"Oh? I guess with all of your experience with younger kids, you can advise me on how to handle her?" Kate suggested snippily.

For almost eleven years, Stephanie's been the only child in the Green family, and now her mom's expecting a baby. Stephanie's hardly ever been around little kids, it's true, but that doesn't stop her from having very definite ideas about how to handle them.

"Wait until you have one living across the hall from you," Kate went on. "Then maybe I'll listen!"

"If I were you, I'd feel complimented!" Stephanie said, as though she hadn't heard Kate. "Imitation is the sincerest form of flattery — Melissa was just trying to be more like you."

"Right," Kate muttered. "I guess that's why she had my glasses on upside down" — Kate's a little nearsighted, although she hardly ever wears her glasses — "my new sneakers on the wrong feet, and was walking like a geek, giggling her silly head off!"

Stephanie was pulling the black-and-white sweatshirt off over her head, so she didn't bother to answer.

"Anyway, Lauren," Kate said to me, "make a list — that way you won't forget anything important."

Kate has been trying to organize me practically since we were babies. She and I live almost next door to each other on Pine Street — there's just one house between us. We started playing together when we were still in diapers. By the time we began kindergarten, we were best friends.

That's when the sleepovers started, too. Every Friday night, either Kate would sleep over at my house, or I would sleep over at hers. Dr. Beekman, Kate's dad, named us the "Sleepover Twins."

We dressed up in our moms' clothes and pretended we were grown-ups, or played Monopoly, or school. We made S'mores in the toaster oven, and Kool-Pops in all the ice-cube trays, using Dr. Beekman's tongue depressors for popsicle sticks.

As we got older, our cooking improved. Kate perfected a recipe for marshmallow super-fudge, and I invented a special onion-soup-olives-bacon-bits-and-sour-cream dip. There were Roger and his friends to spy on — Roger's my older brother — and Melissa the Monster to steer clear of. Kate and I thought up thousands of Mad Libs. We also watched every movie ever shown on TV — Kate would like to be a movie director some day.

We had other friends at school, of course, but for years it was just Kate and me at the sleepovers. Then, the summer before fourth grade, Stephanie Green moved from the city to the other end of Pine Street. I got to know her because we were both in 4A, Mr. Civello's class, last year.

I thought Stephanie was neat. She told great stories about her life back in the city. She knew a lot about the latest styles, and she was a terrific dancer. She was so much fun I decided to ask her to one of our Friday-night sleepovers — I wanted Kate to get to know her, too.

D-I-S-A-S-T-E-R! After that one sleepover, Kate was convinced that Stephanie was a total air-head who could only talk about rock videos and the city. And Stephanie thought Kate was much too serious. In fact, she told me privately that Kate was a stuffy know-it-all!

My brother, Roger, claimed they were too much alike in one big, important way: Each of them was used to telling everybody else what to do.

Maybe Roger was right. Maybe one of the reasons Kate and I have gotten along so well for so many years is that we're completely different. We might have seemed like Sleepover Twins to Dr. Beekman, but that couldn't be farther from the truth. I'm tall, with brown hair; Kate's short and blonde. She's incredibly neat, and I have to admit I can be pretty messy. She's always sensible; I let my imagination run away with me sometimes. She makes me pull myself together, and I think I loosen her up a little.

I'm usually more easygoing than Kate is, but I can be stubborn, too. I wanted Kate and Stephanie to be friends, so I didn't give up.

After Stephanie's first sleepover at my house, she invited Kate and me to spend the night at hers. Mrs. Green baked those fantastic cookies, and we stuffed ourselves with them while we watched a triple-feature on Stephanie's private TV. (Since she's an only child, Stephanie has her own TV, her own VCR, and her own phone — a red princess with a twenty-five-foot cord.)

Before long, Stephanie, Kate, and I started riding our bikes back and forth to school together, and hanging out at the mall or at Charlie's Soda Fountain on Saturdays. Although nobody bothered pointing it out, the Sleepover Twins were slowly and surely becoming a threesome.

It wasn't that Kate and Stephanie had decided to see eye-to-eye. They still came up with plenty to argue about, with me as the only referee . . . until Patti Jenkins turned up in Mrs. Mead's fifth-grade class.

You'd never know it, but Patti's from the city, too. She and Stephanie even went to the same school there for a couple of years, but they couldn't be less alike. Patti's as quiet and shy as Stephanie is bubbly and outgoing. Patti is also kind and thoughtful. She's tall, and she's good at sports, too.

Kate and I both liked Patti right away. School

had barely started this year, when suddenly there were *four* Sleepover Friends!

Stephanie was pulling a pair of brand-new, black stone-washed jeans out of the chest of drawers when the Greens' phone rang. "I'll get it, Mom," she yelled down the hall. "I'll bet it's Molly," Stephanie added to us as she grabbed the phone.

Molly Jones had stayed with Stephanie when the Walden kids visited us, and they'd really hit it off. They'd talked on the phone at least once a week since then. Molly had promised to call as soon as she knew where we'd all be staying in Walden.

"Hello? . . . Molly!" Stephanie shrieked. She held the phone away from her ear so all four of us could hear.

"Hi, Molly!" Kate, Patti, and I shouted.

"Hi, guys," Molly said. "We drew names this afternoon!"

"And?" Stephanie said excitedly.

"You'll be staying with Annette. . . ." Annette Hollis had spent the week with me when the Walden fifth-graders were in Riverhurst.

Stephanie grinned at the rest of us. "The red stretchpants will be just fine — I sure won't be milking cows or slopping hogs at the Hollises'." Annette's dad is *not* a farmer — he's the school superintendent in Walden.

"Rebecca drew Lauren's name. . . ." Molly continued.

"Way to go!" I said. I'd wanted to try out a farm, and Rebecca Newman and her family live on one, along with her grandparents and aunts and uncles and their children. Rebecca is really nice — she'd spent part of her Riverhurst stay with Patti.

Stephanie poked me with her toe. "All right!" she said. It just so happens that Rebecca's cousin Reggie Bennett is *really* cute.

"And . . . Patti's staying with me!" Molly exclaimed.

"Great!" Patti beamed. Molly is lots of fun, and her parents sound cool, too — they're both artists.

So we were all settled except for Kate, who grabbed the phone away from Stephanie. "What about me? Do I get Darlene?" she asked Molly. Darlene Kastner had stayed with Kate in Riverhurst.

Stephanie, Patti, and I couldn't hear what Molly was saying, but we could see Kate's left eyebrow go up.

"Oh . . . Wanda Barnes?" she said. "She didn't come down here when the rest of you did. Mmm-hmmm . . . *five* kids in their family?! You're not

10

serious! . . . Okay . . . Thanks, Molly. Here's Stephanie.''

Kate handed the phone back to Stephanie. She filled us in while Stephanie said good-bye to Molly.

"Darlene drew Jane Sykes," Kate told Patti and me.

"They should get along well," Patti said. Everyone gets along with Jane, and she and Darlene both like sports.

"My name was drawn by a girl named Wanda Barnes," Kate reported. "The Barneses raise some kind of fancy sheep, and Wanda didn't want to come to Riverhurst because it was lambing time."

"Sheep are darling!" Patti said. "They look like little clouds on legs. . . ." Patti loves animals and she's smart — she'd probably make a great veterinarian.

"Yeah, but how darling are Wanda's four brothers and sisters?" Kate said gloomily. "I only have *one* to put up with at my house, and she drives me crazy!"

"Melissa drives you crazy exactly because she's your sister," I told Kate. "You'll be *company* at the Barneses', and Wanda and her parents will keep the kids under control."

"See you Sunday afternoon," Stephanie was

11

saying to Molly. She hung up the phone and joined our conversation. "Five kids! I'm kind of sorry Wanda didn't draw my name — I could try out some of my child-managing ideas!" Stephanie said.

"Oh, yeah?" Kate said to Stephanie. "Just what exactly are those?"

Stephanie folded up the black jeans and squashed them down on the red stretchpants. "Most important," she replied, "is always having a good sense of humor."

"What about being firm? If you give an inch, they'll take a mile," Kate said. "And making up a schedule to keep them busy so they don't have time to dream up ways to get into trouble?"

"Coming up with lots of fun things to do would work a lot better," Stephanie said positively.

Kate raised an eyebrow. She opened her mouth to argue, and then closed it again. "With five kids around, you could try out quite a few of your ideas in a week," Kate said cagily. "Want to trade houses?"

Stephanie thought it over for a minute or two. "I wouldn't want Annette to feel that I'd rather stay with the Barneses," she replied at last.

Before Kate could say anything else, Stephanie's phone rang again. "Molly must have forgotten to tell us something," Stephanie predicted, snatching it up. "Hi!"

But it wasn't Molly after all. "Oh, hello, Mr. Rhodes," Stephanie said. "Is something wrong with Sleepover?" she added quickly.

Chapter 2

Kate, Patti, and I traded worried looks. Sleepover is a donkey. He's a burro, actually, who arrived at Stephanie's house in Riverhurst after growing up on government lands in Arizona.

Whenever I tell anybody this story, Kate always interrupts at this point: "Yes, Lauren, but have you explained exactly how Sleepover *found* the Greens' house all the way from Arizona?"

The answer to that is, I'm not one-hundred percent certain. A month or so ago, Stephanie got the feeling that her parents were keeping an awful secret from her. She decided that her father must have lost his job at Blake, Binder, and Rosten — Mr. Green's a lawyer — and that her family would be running out of money any second. To try to help out, Patti

14

and I looked in magazines and clipped entry blanks for contests with cash prizes. Then we filled in Stephanie's name and address.

I filled out lots of them, and there *is* a chance that, in the shuffle, I accidentally sent in a form to "Friends of the Burro." Friends of the Burro is an organization that puts wild burros up for adoption.

Anyway, it turned out there was nothing wrong with Mr. Green's job. Instead, the secret was about Mrs. Green and the baby. Which gave Stephanie a great line when the burro arrived in her driveway by truck: "It's the perfect baby gift!" she'd said to her parents. "He's cute, and cuddly, and little-kid-sized!"

Sleepover *is* cute. He's a soft grayish-brown, he has enormous brown eyes with thick black lashes, and a clump of curls between his long, furry ears. He's not much bigger than Roger's part-Newfoundland dog, Bullwinkle.

Mr. Green had agreed to keep him until we could find a better home.

We named the burro Sleepover, for the Sleepover Friends. That first day, Sleepover ate all of the flowers in front of the Greens' house and got a good start on the next-door neighbors' shrubs.

"Ron," Mrs. Green had said to her husband.

"I'm sure there are laws against keeping a burro in the yard, and if there aren't, there will be — he's well on his way to turning Pine Street into the Arizona desert. We'd better find a stable for him, quickly!"

But you'd be surprised at how many stables won't have anything to do with a donkey.

"Do you know what that sort of animal would do to our reputation?" said the snooty man we talked to at Carriage House Riding Academy.

The lady at Riverhurst Equestrian Center was just as horrified when we told her about the burro. "I'm afraid not — our horses are much too well-bred and sensitive. A single ear-splitting bray, and their nerves. . . . Need I say more?"

"We have a two-year waiting list," drawled the owner of Deep Hollow Stables. "And since I don't even consider *horses* without pedigrees, a wild donkey is out of the question!"

Sleepover spent the night in the Greens' garage, but he certainly didn't *sleep*. He knocked over Mr. Green's workbench, made a smallish dent in Mrs. Green's car door and kept half of Pine Street awake with his hee-haws.

Mr. Green was trying to find a phone number for Friends of the Burro the next morning — "That donkey needs all the friends he can get right now," he told Stephanie — when Patti called their house. She'd been to the hardware store with her dad, and had spotted a card on the bulletin board: "Rocky Rhodes' Happy Trails Stable, 203 Glendale Avenue."

That afternoon Patti, Kate, and I drove out to Happy Trails with Stephanie and Mr. Green. It's not far off the highway at the south end of Riverhurst. It's kind of a run-down little place, with a small red house in front, and the stable down a dirt road behind it. But Mr. Rocky Rhodes had several empty stalls, and he couldn't have been nicer about boarding a burro.

"No problem," he said as soon as we'd told him about Sleepover. "I've stabled all kinds of things. I had a longhorn cow once, and a billy goat for a couple of years. . . ." He loaned us his trailer to move Sleepover from the Greens' house to the stable.

Sleepover seemed to like his stall, and he made friends right away with the Shetland pony next door. We rode our bikes out to visit him every two or three days and on weekends. We were planning on training him to help us out in the birthday-party business the four of us have. We'd add "burro rides" to our list of services. Everything seemed fine.

But now Mr. Rhodes sounded furious! "I need to talk to your dad, pronto! Is he around?" he growled at Stephanie, loudly enough for the rest of us to hear.

"No — is there something I can do?" she asked.

"Find this donkey of yours a new home!" Mr. Rhodes replied grimly. "Today he kicked a hole in his stall, waltzed out of the stable, crashed through the back door of my house, wrecked the kitchen, ate a cake right off the counter. . . ." Mr. Rhodes had to catch his breath. "When my wife and I got home, he'd made himself comfortable in our living room, and he was chewing on my chaps!"

Mr. Rhodes is very proud of his blue leather Western chaps, which he only wears on special occasions.

"I figure he's done at least three hundred dollars worth of damage," Mr. Rhodes continued. "And if you don't get that burro out of here fast, tell your father I'm charging him interest!" He slammed the phone down with a bang.

"There aren't any other stables in Riverhurst," Patti said anxiously as Stephanie hung up her phone.

"What about looking for one in Dannerville?" I suggested. Dannerville is the next town over.

"We can't ride our bikes to Dannerville. Sleep-over would get terribly lonesome," Stephanie said gloomily. "What are we going to do?"

"There are lots of people with horses who don't

keep them at public stables. Someone is bound to have an extra stall," Kate said. "We could put an ad in the paper."

"We'd never find a place before the weekend," Stephanie said. "I guess I'll have to cancel my week in Walden to stay home and look for — "

The phone rang again, making us all jump.

Stephanie groaned. "I just know it's Mr. Rhodes calling back — I'm not going to answer it."

"Then your mother will, and she won't know what he's talking about," Kate pointed out.

I was nearest, so I picked up the phone on the second ring and spoke in my sternest voice. "Hello!"

"Is this the Greens' residence?" asked a girl on the other end of the line.

"Yes, it is. Who is this?" I said.

"Rebecca Newman."

"Rebecca! It's Lauren!"

"Why did you sound so funny?" Rebecca wanted to know. "Like you were ready to bite some-one's head off."

I told her about our problem with Sleepover. "Stephanie may have to cancel her trip to Walden so she can find him another place to stay." And if she did, so would I. Sleepover probably wouldn't have been with us at all if I'd been paying closer attention to the forms I was filling out. It was only fair for me to keep Stephanie company.

"I've got a better idea," Rebecca said.

"What?" I said.

"*We'll* take him!" she replied.

"You'll keep Sleepover on your farm?" I exclaimed, looking at Stephanie and shrugging my shoulders.

Stephanie nodded yes. "I'll miss him," she murmured, "but I think he might be happier on a farm."

"We have plenty of room in the old horse barn," Rebecca said. "He could sleep there at night, and spend his days outside. And my little sisters would love him!"

"My dad'll pay for his food!" Stephanie called out.

"Tell Stephanie we feed over two hundred cows every day," Rebecca said to me . "I don't think one little burro would make much difference."

"All we have to do is figure out how to get him there." I giggled. "I don't think he can go with us on the bus." The Riverhurst kids were riding to Walden on one of the elementary school buses on Sunday.

"I'll bet Rocky Rhodes would rent us his trailer," Stephanie suggested.

"Actually . . . I was calling to see if you four could possibly drive up here a day early," Rebecca told me. "For a sleepover on Saturday night. And now that the donkey is coming. . . ."

"I'll ask dad to drive us up with Sleepover on Saturday morning!" Stephanie said.

"Will he mind?" Patti asked. "Walden's kind of far away."

"Not after he hears what Rocky Rhodes has to say," Stephanie said. "This'll solve all of our problems."

"It's settled then," Rebecca said. "You're all invited to a big sleepover at my house this Saturday."

Chapter
3

We gave up our usual Friday-night sleepover that week because our parents didn't want us to be totally dragged out by Sunday. "Two sleepovers, plus a long trip, in two days is too much," all our mothers agreed.

I spent the evening packing and unpacking while Kate and I talked about our wardrobes on the telephone. The next morning, she and I met on the sidewalk in front of my house. Kate was wearing a blue-and-yellow striped shirt, denim overalls, and her blue leather sneakers. I was wearing my favorite jeans, a blue-and-green rugby shirt, and silver hightops. Both of us were carrying our suitcases. Kate's was flat and neat, of course, and mine bulged in weird places with last-minute additions.

Kate looked at her watch. "Nine-ten — they should be here any minute with Sleepover." Stephanie and her dad were picking up the burro first.

"Hey, girls — running away from home?"

It was Donald Foster, his head stuck out of his bedroom window. Donald's a seventh-grader and just about the most conceited boy in Riverhurst. Since he lives in the house between Kate's and mine, he's witnessed all kinds of sleepover goings-on, and he never lets us forget it. Seeing us taking off with a burro would make his day.

"No!" I said firmly. "It's awfully early — don't you want to get your beauty rest?"

"Too late," Kate said in a low voice. "Hear the trailer?"

Sure enough, I heard a clanking sound in the distance, growing louder and louder as we listened.

Mr. Green's car turned the corner off Hillcrest onto Pine Street. The car was going slowly, but the trailer was jumping up and down behind it as though it had a life of its own. It does have a life of its own, I thought, and said out loud, "Sleepover!"

"I know!" Donald shouted as soon as he spotted the donkey in the trailer. "You're joining a traveling circus!"

"Cute!" Kate muttered. "Very cute!"

Mr. Green pulled over to the curb next to us and braked. The trailer kept rocking and rolling as Sleepover hopped backward and forward inside it.

Stephanie leaped out of the car to poke some apple slices between the wooden slats on the side of the trailer. "Hi, guys," she said to us. She was wearing her red-and-black-checked jumpsuit and short black boots. "Hey, Donald!" she yelled. Stephanie's not easily embarrassed, and besides, she agrees with Donald — she thinks he's great-looking, too.

"What's wrong with Sleepover?" I asked her. "He didn't act like this on his way *over* to Happy Trails."

Stephanie fed the burro more apple slices and stroked his nose. "Poor sweetie," she said. "Happy Trails wasn't a good experience for him."

"Or for me," said Mr. Green, patting his wallet. He opened the trunk of the car. "Let's load your suitcases, girls, and make our getaway, before our fuzzy friend here decides to. . . ."

Sleepover finished the apple slices and asked for more with a full-volume hee-haw. Down at the end of the block, Mrs. Norris was walking her dog, Barney. Barney got so freaked out by the noise that he dragged Mrs. Norris straight into the lilac hedge.

Donald was laughing so hard he almost fell out the window.

"Next I'll be fined for disturbing the peace," Mr. Green said grimly.

He threw our suitcases on top of Stephanie's three red ones. "Three suitcases for a week?" Kate murmured to me, and all of us piled into the car.

"Bye!" Donald called out. "See you under the big top!"

My parents waved from the front door as we pulled away, to the sounds of clanking and braying.

We swung by Patti's house, where we didn't have to honk. Sleepover announced our arrival, loud and clear. Patti squeezed into the backseat with Kate and me, and Mr. Green headed north.

"Two hundred and seventeen miles," Kate informed us. "I figured it out in the atlas last night."

"I'll have to drive fairly slowly with the trailer behind us," Mr. Green said. "The trip should take at least five-and-a-half hours, plus some time for lunch. . . ."

"I'm hungry already," I admitted. The peanut butter and jelly on an English muffin that I'd eaten for breakfast was a distant memory.

"I thought we might be, so I brought snacks," Stephanie said, leaning over to reach into a big paper bag at her feet. "Caramel popcorn, mixed nuts, chocolate-covered raisins. . . ."

"And I brought some sugar cookies," said Patti, opening her canvas tote.

Stephanie turned the radio on so we could listen to WBRM, a Riverhurst station, and we passed food back and forth while we talked about the stuff we'd be doing in Walden.

"We should get there around the middle of the afternoon," Stephanie said. "I think there'll be time for Rebecca to show us around Walden before dinner."

"Speaking of dinner," Patti said, "on Saturday night, all of Rebecca's family eats together at her grandparents' house. Fifteen people, not counting visitors. They usually have at least two kinds of meat and home-grown vegetables and real biscuits and lots of desserts. . . ."

"I can't wait!" I said. "More popcorn back here, please, Stephanie."

After about an hour, Sleepover had calmed down a little.

"I think he may be sleeping," Patti said, peering at the trailer through the back window.

I was getting kind of drowsy myself. It was warm in the car, Mr. Green had lowered the volume on

26

the radio, and there was nothing but rocks and trees to look at on the interstate.

I guessed I dozed off, because I dreamed about a huge farm dinner that I ate all by myself. With each mouthful, I got fatter. By the time I was finished, I looked like the Goodyear blimp!

My eyes flew open as the car stopped. I felt one of my legs. It was as skinny as usual. My imagination again, I thought. All because of Stephanie talking about blowing up like a balloon.

We were parked on the shoulder of the highway, and Stephanie was opening her door. "What's wrong?" I asked.

"Sleepover started bouncing again," Stephanie answered. "And Kate was feeling carsick, so we're changing places."

Stephanie moved into the backseat with Patti and me, and Kate sat in front with Mr. Green. "A soda would probably settle your stomach," he told Kate as we pulled onto the road again. "All of you keep your eyes peeled for a place to stop."

Not five minutes later, Stephanie and I both called out, "Woody's Gas, Bait, and Food!"

"That ought to cover it," said Mr. Green, turning into the parking lot.

We scrambled out of the car and headed for the

27

gray-shingled building on the other side of a row of gas pumps.

Sleepover gave the trailer a kick as we walked by.

"I'll buy you something if you're good," Stephanie murmured through the slats.

Sleepover kicked the trailer even harder.

"It won't work any better with kids," Kate giggled, and Stephanie made a face.

Woody's store was one of those places that sells a little bit of everything, like postcards of giant trout, sunglasses, sandwiches, baseball caps, and fishing tackle.

Stephanie, Kate, and I grabbed Dr Peppers, and Mr. Green had just paid for them and for a double-dip fudge-ripple ice-cream cone for Patti when the lady behind the counter exclaimed, "I declare! There's a donkey at the gas pumps!"

The four of us and Mr. Green were out the door in a flash!

Sleepover was standing next to one of the Super Unleaded pumps, nibbling lazily at the hose and watching the traffic go by.

"Slow down — we don't want him to run out onto the highway," Mr. Green said quietly. "Lauren, you and Patti sneak around the back of the store and

28

get in front of him." Mr. Green chose us because we're faster than Kate and Stephanie. "When you're in position, the three of us will move closer, too — we'll kind of pen Sleepover up between the rows of pumps."

"Could you hold my ice cream?" Patti said to Stephanie, since we were going to have to run.

"Take it!" Stephanie told her. "Sleepover loves sweets — remember Mr. Rhodes' cake?"

Patti and I crept along the front of the building until we got to the side. Then we raced around the back and the other side. We walked slowly out in front of Sleepover, Patti holding her ice-cream cone up in the air like the Statue of Liberty's torch.

"Good Sleepover," she said. "Nice Sleep-over — you don't want to run away from us, do you?"

He didn't. He strolled right up to us and let us grab his halter.

"Whew!" I said.

"Good work, guys!" Stephanie and Kate hurried over, and Mr. Green took the halter lead.

He led Sleepover back to the trailer. "Look at this!" Mr. Green said, pointing to the thick nylon rope he'd used to tie the trailer gate closed. It was chewed right through! "I think Houdini would have been a better name for this animal. Okay, Sleepover — back inside."

He pointed Sleepover at the trailer and gave him a slap on the rump. The donkey wouldn't move, except to raise his nose and sniff in the direction of Patti's fudge-ripple cone.

"Now what's wrong?" Mr. Green sighed. He walked into the trailer himself and stuck the end of the halter lead through the slats in front. "Two of us will pull on the lead, two of us will push on the donkey — "

"And Patti will use her ice cream as a bribe!" Stephanie said.

"Okay," we all agreed.

Patti climbed into the trailer; Mr. Green jumped out. Kate and I grabbed the end of Sleepover's halter lead, and Mr. Green and Stephanie got behind the donkey.

"Pull on the lead!" Mr. Green called out over the noise of the traffic whizzing past on the highway.

While Patti dangled her double-dip fudge-ripple in front of Sleepover's furry nose, Kate and I tugged as hard as we could on the lead.

"Push!" Kate shouted to Stephanie and Mr. Green.

Stephanie and her dad pushed with all their might on Sleepover's other end.

Just then, a huge oil truck rumbled into the gas station, and the driver gave a couple of sharp blasts on his horn.

I don't know if Sleepover was desperate for fudge-ripple ice cream, or if the truck scared him, but suddenly he shot into the trailer like a rocket.

Before the donkey could change his mind and back out, Mr. Green had slammed the trailer door shut.

"We did it!" Kate and Stephanie and I squealed.

"I'll tie it shut, Dad," Stephanie told Mr. Green, grabbing one of the longer pieces of nylon rope.

"Not this time," Mr. Green said firmly. "This time we're going to padlock it shut. I think I've got a bike lock in the trunk of my car. . . ."

"Would you mind getting me out of here first?" a muffled voice asked.

We'd been so busy congratulating ourselves, we'd forgotten Patti!

Chapter 4

After the excitement at Woody's, the rest of our trip was pretty calm. We stopped at a drive-in just long enough to grab some burgers and more sodas. Sleepover tried to bite through Mr. Green's bike lock while we were parked, but even *his* teeth aren't that strong.

We listened to WBRM until we got too far away from Riverhurst to pick up the signal. When we switched to WNXS–Hamilton, we knew we were getting closer to Walden, since Hamilton is the nearest big town.

At about three o'clock that afternoon, we passed a road sign that said Walden — 11 miles. Everybody clapped, and Mr. Green tooted his horn. The countryside had changed from pine trees and rocky hills to rolling pastures and giant wooden barns.

"Do you have the directions to Rebecca's house?" Kate asked Stephanie.

"First we drive straight through Walden," Stephanie said.

We rolled over a hill and into the town, down a street lined with old shingled houses and huge trees. It turned into Main Street, and we drove past some of the places the Walden kids had told us about.

"Look, the Doughnut Hole!" Kate pointed out. Their doughnuts are made to order, and Rebecca and Darlene stop by sometimes on Saturdays.

"And Star Confectionery," I said. "Tuna melts and hot butterscotch sundaes." The Star was Annette's favorite place.

"An old-fashioned general store," said Mr. Green as we stopped at the single traffic light. Albright's big plate-glass window was piled with everything from a stuffed moose head to a canoe. A poster for a circus was squeezed into one corner.

Sleepover was clattering around in the trailer again, but no one walking on the street paid much attention. I guess in Walden noisy animals in trailers are nothing unusual.

"Here comes the school!" said Kate when we started moving again.

The high school and junior high were on our right, with a big bronze eagle-and-flag statue out front. The elementary school was across the road.

"It's bigger than I thought it would be," Stephanie said about the building. "The town is so little."

"Walden is small, but there are lots of kids living outside of town on farms," Patti reminded her.

"Now where do we go?" Mr. Green asked Stephanie. "We're running out of Walden."

"Oh — yeah." Stephanie pulled a slip of paper out of her pocket and read it quickly. "Uh — we're supposed to keep going for three miles, until we see a wagon wheel next to a white iron gate, on the right side of the road. . . ."

It wasn't hard to find. We drove through the gate and up a graveled lane to a yellow three-story house with oak trees on either side of it. We'd barely stopped when Rebecca ran down the front steps.

She was followed by two collies, two little girls in jeans, a tall man wearing a green flannel shirt and overalls, and a pretty woman with her brown hair in a French braid.

"You made it!" Rebecca called out.

As we climbed out of the car, she introduced her parents — "Carlton," her father added to Mr. Green, "and this is my wife, Annemarie" — and her two little sisters, Tracy, an eight-year-old with straight blonde hair, and six-year-old Janis, who has brown curls. The two dogs were George and Martha, and they stopped jumping on us as soon as Mr. Newman said, "Sit."

"Maybe Bullwinkle should come up here for a month or two," I said to Kate. "Pick up a few tips." Bullwinkle will knock you down flat nine times out of ten.

"So this is the famous burro," Mr. Newman said, looking through the slats of the trailer at Sleepover. "All the way from Arizona."

"That's right," said Mr. Green, putting a key in the bike lock and clicking it open. "He chews through ropes," he explained to Mr. Newman.

Sleepover backed hurriedly out of the trailer as soon as he heard the creak of the gate. Then he just stood there, sniffing the air and checking everything out.

"Oh, Daddy — he's sweet!" Tracy said, throwing her arms around the burro's neck.

"His face is so soft!" said Janis, patting Sleepover's nose. "I think he looks hungry."

"Let's feed him!" Tracy said. "We have carrots for him and sugar cubes and — "

"I have a feeling he's going to be very happy here," said Stephanie.

"We'll get him fixed up in the barn first," Mr. Newman told the little girls. "Then you can feed him."

The three of them led Sleepover toward a group of farm buildings.

"Let's go inside, shall we?" Mrs. Newman said to Mr. Green and the rest of us.

"Got any suitcases you need help with?" a new voice asked.

Stephanie jabbed me so hard with her elbow, I got a stitch in my side. It was Rebecca's cousin Reggie Bennett, also known as The Hunk!

"Hi, Reggie," all of us said at the same time.

Reggie has spiky blond hair, pale blue eyes, and a great smile. He's the kind of guy everybody agrees is terrific-looking. That day he was wearing an electric-blue sweater, faded jeans, and work boots.

Reggie's basically shy. As cute as he is, he's not a bit vain. Kate says he *has* to be nearsighted — if he weren't, he'd either see himself in the mirror, or

36

notice girls dropping dead over him, or both, and be as conceited as Donald Foster.

"Sure, Reggie," Rebecca was saying to her cousin. "The suitcases are all going up to the third floor."

Stephanie opened the trunk of her dad's car. Reggie took two suitcases; Stephanie, Rebecca, Kate, Patti, and I one each. We followed Rebecca into the front hall of her house, and up a long flight of stairs to the second-floor landing. Then we climbed a shorter flight to the third floor.

We stepped into a narrow room with windows at either end looking out on the barns, a pond, and three more houses. Two little bedrooms were tucked under the eaves, with glass doors between them.

"Just put your stuff down in any empty space," she said.

That wasn't so easy to do, since both rooms were almost filled, wall to wall, with beds and cots.

"Wow!" said Stephanie. "*How* many people live here?"

"Just the ones you met," Rebecca said with a laugh. "These rooms don't usually look like this, but we borrowed all the spare beds on the farm for the sleepover tonight."

"Who's coming?" Kate asked.

"Well . . . Molly and Annette — they'll be over in a little while — Darlene, too," Rebecca replied.

Along with Rebecca, these were the four girls who stayed with us in Riverhurst.

"We've been taking turns having sleepovers almost every Friday," Rebecca went on.

"The Walden branch of the Sleepover Friends," Patti said, smiling.

"Right!" said Rebecca. "And I invited Wanda Barnes, too."

"You're staying at the Barneses', aren't you?" Reggie asked Kate.

"Yes," Kate said.

Reggie grinned. "Keep your eye on Will — he's *something*."

"Who's Will?" I asked.

"The eight-year-old — he's my little brother's age, and is he wild!" Reggie answered.

"Oh, great!" Kate groaned.

"Of course, the twins aren't exactly relaxing, either," Reggie went on.

"Twins!" Kate exclaimed, horrified.

"Mandy and Thomas," Reggie said. "They're seven."

"That makes four kids, with Wanda," Stephanie said. "I thought there were five."

"Don't remind me," Kate murmured.

"There are — Frank's the oldest. He's fifteen," Rebecca said.

"He's the best wrestler at Walden High," Reggie added.

"Sounds perfect," said Kate. "Three monsters and the Incredible Hulk."

"Don't worry, Kate — Mrs. Barnes keeps them in line at home," Rebecca told her. "Mrs. Barnes is very strict."

A horn honked outside. Rebecca ran to the window. "It's Wanda," she said. "Let's go downstairs."

We were waiting on the porch when the Barneses' green station wagon stopped in front of the house. Rebecca's mom had stepped outside, too.

"Hello, hello!" said the man driving. He was big and balding, he seemed determined to be cheerful, and he had a booming voice. He jumped out of the car and gave us all a big grin.

"Hello, Annemarie," he said to Mrs. Newman. "Which of these little ladies is going to be our guest?"

"Kate Beekman," Mrs. Newman said, putting her arm around Kate's shoulders.

Five kids had climbed out of the station wagon.

They were very different sizes — from about six feet down to about four — three boys and two girls, but they looked surprisingly alike. All of them had pale skin, pale blond hair, and pale blue eyes.

"They're like the kids in *Alien Village*," I murmured to Rebecca. *Alien Village* is a science-fiction TV series about blond mutant children from the planet Zarkon who take over a small town.

Rebecca covered up a giggle with a cough. "Hi, Wanda," she managed to say to the older girl, who had joined us on the porch. "This is Patti Jenkins and Lauren Hunter and Stephanie Green, and that's Kate Beekman."

"Hi, Kate, Patti, Lauren, Stephanie. Glad to meet you." Wanda had a nice smile, but she ducked her head shyly when she talked.

"Where's your mom?" Rebecca asked her.

"She's with my grandmother, over in Hamilton," said Wanda. "Granny's sick, so Mom's staying with her for a few days. . . ." Her voice trailed off.

Kate and I glanced at each other, and Kate rolled her eyes. What had Rebecca told us? "Don't worry, Kate, Mrs. Barnes keeps the kids in line." But what happens when Mrs. Barnes isn't around?

"Mandy, Thomas — get out of Mrs. Newman's

flowers," Mr. Barnes boomed. But he went back to talking to Rebecca's mom, and the little girl and boy kept marching in and out of the flowerbed. Frank was slouched in the car, playing the radio. He didn't even look up.

Wanda smiled apologetically, then gazed anxiously around. "Where's Will?" she asked us.

"I saw him get out of the car," Rebecca answered, "but I didn't notice where he went."

"Mandy, Thomas!" Wanda called softly.

"Take that! And that!" Now the twins were hacking away at Mrs. Newman's marigolds with some branches they'd pulled off a lilac bush.

Wanda ran down the steps and picked up Thomas. His arms and legs kept whacking and stamping, even after she'd lifted him off the ground. "Where . . . is . . . Will?" she repeated. Definitely *Alien Village*.

"He went to the barn!" Thomas wriggled angrily. "Give me air!"

Wanda set Thomas down on the front steps and hurried toward the big white barn. Rebecca, Patti, Kate, Stephanie, and I were right behind her.

The barn's heavy, sliding door was closed, and Wanda whirled in a circle. No Will. Rebecca opened the door a crack and peeked in.

41

Wanda found him pretty fast. He was crouching on the far side of the barn, holding three or four colored markers in his hand and scrawling an enormous, dark purple W on the spotless white wall of the barn.

"Hey, cut that out!" Rebecca yelled, but he'd finished the W, and started on the i in bright red before Wanda reached him. She grabbed his arm just as he stretched to dot the i.

"You're hurting me!" Will whined, his lower lip starting to quiver. "I'm littler than you are. I'll tell Daddy!"

Wanda turned him loose, and she actually started to apologize! "I'm sorry, Will, but you know . . . ," she began.

In a flash, Will dotted the i with a lopsided star and stuck his tongue out at all of us. "Fooled you!" he snickered, and he dashed behind the barn, dropping markers as he went.

"Sorry," Wanda said again, this time to Rebecca.

"Yeah . . . well. . . ," Rebecca said. She touched the ragged letters. "Dad's going to love this. He just painted the barn last week." Rebecca turned and walked angrily back to the house.

"So Will's artistic!" Stephanie said brightly to Wanda.

Kate looked at Patti and me, tight-lipped, and rolled her eyes.

I had a feeling that Kate's ideas for child-control, like being firm, and keeping kids on a schedule, would definitely be put to the test that week!

Chapter 5

Wanda didn't stay for dinner or the sleepover that evening. Maybe she felt funny about Will's graffiti, or maybe she thought her dad needed her help with the younger kids.

"No need for Kate to miss the party, though," Mr. Barnes boomed at Mrs. Newman. "We'll visit Granny Mercer in the morning, and pick Kate up on our way home tomorrow afternoon."

"That'll be fine," said Mrs. Newman. "Kate is welcome here for as long as she likes."

"How about a week?" Kate murmured to Patti and me under her breath. "Even Melissa could learn a few nasty tricks from the Barnes monsters."

Stephanie's dad left before dinner, too — he had a long drive home.

But even without him, there were twenty-two people in Grandpa and Grandma Newman's dining room. Fifteen regulars, which included Rebecca, her parents and little sisters; Grandma and Grandpa Newman; Rebecca's Uncle Jeff and Aunt Maureen Newman and their baby, Sally; Reggie and his parents, Harley and Carolyn Bennett; plus his little brother, David, and his little sister, Bess. Then there were the four of us from Riverhurst, plus Annette, Molly, and Darlene.

And the food! Grandma and Grandpa Newman have an oak dining table that runs from one end of the room to the other, with benches on either side, each long enough to seat ten people. The table was absolutely piled with things to eat. Rebecca's mom had cooked an enormous ham, Grandma Newman a pot roast, and Aunt Carolyn a huge platter of fried chicken. There were four kinds of vegetables, plus fresh french fries — not out of bags — and three kinds of home-baked bread.

Kate, Darlene, and Reggie sat together near Reggie's dad at one end of the table. They're all science-fiction freaks, and they wanted to talk about a sci-fi movie they'd seen on TV. Annette, Molly, and Stephanie were sitting near Grandma Newman at the other end of the table.

"I'm not exactly the perfect type for a model," Molly was saying as she loaded up her plate. She's about Stephanie's size, with black hair in a braid and round red glasses. "Secretly, Mom wishes I were tall and thin." Mrs. Jones designs clothes for kids.

"Somebody's going to have to *roll* me back to Rebecca's," Stephanie said, digging in.

Patti and I ended up sitting between Grandma Newman and Uncle Jeff; and if one of them wasn't serving us seconds of something, the other was.

"I like a child with a healthy appetite," Grandma Newman would say before she heaped more fried chicken on my plate.

"Farmers have to keep their strength up," said Uncle Jeff, spooning out more creamed onions for me. I had never eaten so much in my life . . . but somehow I found room for a slice of coconut cake and a sliver of lemon pie.

When we'd finally finished, Reggie left for the barn to do his chores. The Newmans wouldn't let us help with the dishes.

"Not tonight," Rebecca's mom said. "I know you girls all want to get settled."

"You'll be helping out plenty for the rest of the week," Grandma Newman said to me. "And we've got four perfectly good kids right here to clear the table — Tracy, Janis, David, and Bess. Now take the rest of the cake" — she handed Rebecca a second coconut cake, which hadn't even been cut — "and get started on your slumber party."

"Sleepover, Grandma," Rebecca said.

"Sleepover," said Grandma Newman.

"Good night," all the aunts and uncles said, and the four Riverhurst girls and the four Walden girls started for Rebecca's house in the twilight.

The barn loomed over us like a huge gray shadow. An owl floated overhead like a giant moth. With the breeze rustling the leaves in the trees, it was really kind of spooky.

Kate didn't help any by saying, "Hey, Rebecca, remember that ghost story you told us when you were in Riverhurst?"

" 'The White Hand'?" Rebecca asked.

Rebecca had told us a very creepy story about something that had happened when her great-great-grandmother was a girl. A farmer and his wife were haunted by a fat, white hand. And I mean *just* a hand. It wasn't attached to a body, not even to an arm. When it first appeared, it tapped on the windows of the farmhouse, frightening the young wife half to death. Soon it was banging on the front door, as if it were trying to get in.

The next thing the farmer and his wife knew, the tapping — and the hand — *were* inside. The wife started having horrible nightmares that she was being strangled . . . and finally, she was strangled! By the *fat, white hand*!

"Thanks for reminding us, Kate," I muttered. As I've said, sometimes my imagination runs away with me, and nothing is guaranteed to start it galloping faster than a ghost story.

"You really believe it?" Stephanie asked Rebecca. She and Kate always make a big deal about how ghost stories don't bother them. In fact, Stephanie thinks scary movies are *funny*!

"Grandma Newman says it's true," Rebecca answered. "She's the one who first told me about it."

"I heard the story from my great-aunt," Darlene said. "The farm's just down the road from here."

"Not the house — the house burned down a long time ago," Rebecca said. "But see that shed on the hill over there?" She stopped near the big white barn to point it out.

I could just make out a gray square against the night sky.

"That shed's on the old Parker farm," Rebecca went on. "Parker was the name of the people who were haunted."

A shiver ran up my spine. "Could we talk about something else, like — " I began, when I was interrupted by a hideous shriek right behind me!

Patti and I both screamed — she's got plenty of imagination herself — and so did Annette. The other girls just giggled: The shriek wasn't a blast from the past from the Parkers' ghost, it was only the sound of the barn door sliding open.

"Hi," Reggie said, stepping around it. "What's so funny?"

"Lauren and Patti and Annette are a little jumpy," Rebecca explained.

"Being out in the country probably takes some getting used to," Reggie said, which I thought was very nice of him. "Does anybody want to see the calves?" he asked us. "Fourteen of them, only a month old."

"No, I'm going on to the house," Rebecca answered. "I want to put this cake down — it's getting heavy."

Darlene, Molly, and Annette had already visited the calves at a sleepover a couple of weeks earlier. They went with Rebecca, and so did Kate. She was anxious to find out if a movie she'd planned to watch in Riverhurst was being shown in Walden.

"Are there any bulls in there?" Stephanie asked.

I guess she'd remembered Kate's warning, and she *was* wearing *red*-and-black checks.

Reggie looked a little puzzled, but he shook his head.

So Stephanie, Patti, and I followed Reggie inside the barn. It was an enormous open space, and it smelled like hay and oats and . . . cows.

"Wow! I've never seen so many cows!" Stephanie exclaimed. "They're so big . . . and they're wearing my colors!"

The cows were lined up in their stalls, flicking their tails happily back and forth as they munched on their dinner. Every single one had large black and white spots.

Reggie grinned. "They're those colors because they're Holsteins," he explained. "Holsteins are one of the best kinds of dairy cattle, and they're always black and white."

"Like Dalmatians," Stephanie said.

"Yeah," said Reggie doubtfully. "Sort of. . . ."

"Well, if I ever want to buy a cow, I'll know what kind to get," Stephanie said.

He led us down an aisle between two rows of Holsteins. "The calves are in here."

He walked into a separate, small room divided

into little square pens, with a calf in each one.

The calves were sleeping, lying on their stomachs with their necks stretched out and their legs curled under them.

"I'm in charge of the calves, along with Uncle Jeff," Reggie said proudly. As we tiptoed out, he switched off the overhead lights. I stood there for a second, and I could hear them snoring softly.

"Where is Sleepover staying?" Stephanie asked as we headed back through the barn.

"In the old horse barn," Reggie answered. "Come on, I'll show you."

"Grandpa kept the plow horses here when he first bought the farm," Reggie explained. "Now we use it to store some of the equipment."

We squeezed through a side door and walked around a green tractor and a large iron triangle with prongs sticking out of it. Reggie told us it was a cultivator. Sleepover was in a wooden stall at the end of the barn. As soon as he saw us, he turned his back.

"Glad to see you, too," said Stephanie.

"He has at least twice as much space here as he did at Happy Trails," Patti said.

"And it's ten times nicer," I added. The stall had

just been painted, the floor was covered with fresh hay, and Sleepover even had his own window to look out of.

"In the daytime, he'll be able to exercise out in the pasture, the kids'll play with him. . . . Sleepover should be in donkey heaven, once he settles down." Reggie stuck his hand into the rubber feed trough. "He didn't eat his dinner — probably all the excitement of his trip." He jiggled the latch on the stall door to make sure it was hooked. "I'll walk you to Rebecca's," Reggie said.

Chapter
6

A sleepover at a farmer's house is more like a sleepover at a doctor's house than you might think. Dr. Beekman often goes to bed early because he's been up all the night before, working at the hospital. And Rebecca's dad goes to bed early because he has to get up at four-thirty or five in the morning to milk the Holsteins, even on weekends. In both places, you have to be fairly quiet from about nine P.M. on. On the plus side, you have the house more or less to yourselves, because the adults are asleep.

We hung out on the third floor until Mr. and Mrs. Newman and Tracy and Janis had come home and settled into their bedrooms for the night. There was plenty for us to do up there, like making up eight beds, and the Riverhurst group showing the Walden group the clothes we'd brought for the week, and talking about where everybody else in Mrs. Mead's class would be staying during the visit.

"Who got Angela Kemp?" Stephanie asked the Walden girls.

"Carol Harrison," Annette answered.

Carol had stayed with Jane Sykes in Riverhurst, and we had gotten to know her.

"Poor Carol," Kate said, because Carol is nice, and Angela Kemp is awful, although not quite as awful as her best and only friend, Jenny Carlin.

"Maybe when she's away from Jenny, Angela will act differently," Patti suggested. Angela is definitely Jenny's sidekick, and not the other way around — she does everything Jenny tells her to do.

Kate and Stephanie shook their heads. "Don't count on it," Stephanie said. "Once a drip, always a drip."

"Why isn't Jenny coming?" Darlene asked.

"She told Mrs. Mead that her grandfather was flying up from Florida, and that she hadn't seen him in ages, and that she couldn't possibly leave Riverhurst while he was there," Kate replied. "But *I* think . . ."

". . . she's still mad at you, Rebecca, for moving

out of her house!" Stephanie finished with a grin.

Jenny Carlin had drawn Rebecca's name before the Walden kids' visit. But Rebecca had found Jenny to be so snooty and catty, not to mention boy-crazy and conceited, that she'd ended up walking out on her, and finishing up her visit at Patti's.

Rebecca shrugged. "So Jenny Carlin hates me." She giggled. "At least I'm in good company."

Jenny hates Kate, Stephanie, Patti, and me, too — especially me, because a boy she liked at the beginning of the school year, Pete Stone, decided to like me for a while. Jenny has never forgiven me for it, although I certainly didn't *do* anything. I mostly avoid Pete now.

Stephanie must have been thinking along the same lines, because she asked the Walden girls, "Where is Pete Stone staying?"

"With Austin Albers," Molly answered.

"The Alberses' farm is on the same bus route as ours," Rebecca told me. "Pete'll be on our bus."

"So will Angela," Darlene pointed out. "Carol Harrison takes your bus, too."

"Wonderful," I said. "Trapped on a bus with Pete Stone and Jenny's personal spy."

"Don't worry," Rebecca said. "Reggie and I will

55

protect you, and so will Kate. The Barnes kids take the same bus — their farm is only a couple of miles up the road.''

"It's going to be one, big, happy family,'' Kate said, raising an eyebrow. She didn't say anything else about the Barneses. I'm sure she wanted to forget about them for as long as she could.

"Let's go down and get something to drink,'' Rebecca said. "Dad stopped at the Beverage Barn and bought two cases of Dr Pepper and Cheetos and Cheese Doodles and sour-cream potato chips and. . . .''

When it comes to refreshments, these farm families really do things right! We tiptoed down the two flights of stairs, and down the hall to the kitchen.

The Newmans have a big, old-fashioned farmhouse kitchen, with lots of wooden cabinets, and plenty of space for a double-doored refrigerator, and a separate giant freezer, too. While Rebecca was getting glasses out of the cabinets, and Darlene was taking ice out of the freezer, I felt a tiny twinge of hunger. Refrigerators set off my appetite alarm. I've probably spent a thousand hours scrounging through the Beekmans'.

"Rebecca,'' I asked casually, "would you mind if I looked through your fridge?''

"Lauren!" Kate scolded.

"How could you even think about food after that dinner?" Stephanie groaned, clutching her stomach. But I'd noticed her sticking a finger into the icing on the coconut cake that was sitting on the counter.

"I wouldn't mind at all," Rebecca said, opening the refrigerator doors for me. "Help yourself." She handed me a plate.

On a scale of one to ten, the Newmans' leftovers were at least a nine. Barbecued spare ribs, stuffed sweet potatoes, macaroni salad. I took a little spoonful of this and that. When Stephanie puffed out her cheeks at me, I said, "I'll jog tomorrow — no problem."

Rebecca loaded a couple of trays with Dr Peppers and chips and cake, and we went into the living room. George and Martha were asleep in a corner. They barely bothered to wag their feathery tails.

"Want to watch some TV?" Rebecca asked us.

"There really isn't much on but reruns," Kate said, disappointed that her movie wasn't being shown on the Walden channel.

"What about Mad Libs?" said Annette.

So we played a few games, until Molly suggested, "Truth or Dare!"

"All ri-i-ight!" everybody agreed.

"My turn first," said Molly. She looked around the room. "Kate, truth or dare?"

"Oh . . . truth," Kate answered, probably thinking that Molly wouldn't get personal.

But Molly asked, "Which boy in Riverhurst do you like the most?"

Kate turned bright red. *I* knew who it was, but I wasn't sure if Kate would answer. Of course, if you don't answer the question in Truth or Dare, you might have to do something truly awful. . . .

Kate stuck to the rules. "Royce Mason," she mumbled at last.

"Royce Mason!" Stephanie screeched. "You never told me that!"

"Who is Royce Mason?" Darlene asked.

"He's a seventh-grader," Stephanie said. "Lauren, did you know about this?"

I shrugged my shoulders, and Stephanie frowned at me.

"What does he look like?" Rebecca asked.

"He's really cute," Patti said. "He has curly brown hair and brown eyes, and he's on the junior high soccer team."

"Is he related to Sally Mason?" Annette wanted to know. Sally's in our class, and Annette had met her in Riverhurst.

"Sally's his sister," I answered.

"It's my turn," Kate interrupted, the blush fading a little. "Uh . . . Darlene, truth or dare?"

Darlene chose truth.

"Who's the first boy you ever kissed?" Kate asked.

Darlene giggled. "Marlon Dinkins," she answered.

"Marlon Dinkins!" Annette yelped.

"Gross me out!" said Rebecca.

"*Eeeeuuu*. Darlene!" Molly said. "Yuck!"

"Marlon Dinkins is the biggest goody-goody in Walden," Rebecca explained. "He's been the teacher's pet since kindergarten."

"Not to mention the fact that he's really tall and only weighs about forty pounds," added Molly.

"And half of that is the grease he puts on his hair," said Annette.

"I was only four at the time," Darlene said in her own defense.

"Glad to hear it!" said Rebecca. "I thought you were losing touch with reality — too many sci-fi movies."

The game hopped around from person to person for a while, until finally it was Stephanie's turn. I was certain she would call on me, and she did.

"Lauren . . . ," she said slowly, ". . . truth . . . or dare?"

I knew if I said "truth," she would ask me something totally embarrassing. And how bad could a dare be, out here on the farm?

"Dare," I said.

How bad could it be? The answer is, *pretty bad.* Stephanie smiled craftily. "Walk to the shed on the Parker farm, go inside, stay there for two minutes, and come back," she said. Obviously she was *really* annoyed that I'd never told her about Royce Mason.

"Are you crazy?" I practically shrieked. Just thinking about it made those barbecued spare ribs jump around in my stomach.

"You won't be alone," Stephanie told me. "I'll go with you — to make sure you do it!"

"I'm sure the Newmans wouldn't want us wandering around the farm at night," I said, hoping somebody would back me up.

But Darlene said, "Nobody would know. Everyone's asleep."

Rebecca said, "I'll go, too, so you won't fall in the pond or something. I've been to the shed a bunch of times . . . in the daylight, of course," she added in a lower voice.

"You chose the dare, Lauren," Stephanie reminded me.

"I know, I know," I said crossly. "Do I at least get a flashlight?"

"We don't need one. The moon is shining brightly enough," said Stephanie. "Is everybody ready?"

All of us walked into the kitchen. Rebecca pushed open the back door and stepped outside on the porch. "Sssh," she warned. "Stay right behind me."

Chapter
7

Kate, Patti, Annette, Darlene, and Molly huddled together at the door. Stephanie and I followed Rebecca single file: me first and then Stephanie. We hurried across the Newmans' backyard and out the gate. Then we crept between Reggie's house and Grandma and Grandpa Newman's. We crossed a small fenced pasture behind the houses. We climbed through the fence, cut through a row of birches, and started up the hill toward the Parker shed.

"I can't believe you're making us do this, Stephanie," I whispered over my shoulder at her.

"I can't believe you didn't tell me about Royce Mason!" she hissed back.

"What if Patti or I told you something, and swore

you to secrecy," I said. "Would you tell Kate?"

"Of course not," Stephanie replied after a second or two.

"So?" I said to her.

"Yeah . . . well . . . I guess I see what you mean," she admitted at last.

"Fine." I stopped walking. "Then let's turn around."

"Are you going back?" Rebecca said from a few steps up the hill.

"We've already gone this far. . . ." Stephanie nudged me forward.

We jumped over a low stone fence, walked around a little pine grove, and there it was: the ghostly shed!

"Here we are," said Rebecca a little breathlessly. After all, she sort of *believed* in the ghost.

"Nothing to it," said Stephanie, reaching out for the door. It was kind of lopsided, hanging by only one set of hinges. She had a hard time making it move, but she was determined, and finally she tugged it open.

"After you," Stephanie said to me.

I really thought I was going to keel over with fright. My feet seemed to have frozen to the ground — I couldn't move them at all.

Rebecca took a deep breath. "I'll go first," she said.

That made me get a grip on myself, because I knew that Rebecca was scared, too. I managed to unlock my knees enough to shuffle through the door behind her.

The shed didn't have any windows to let in the moonlight, so it was pitch-black inside, except for right around the door. It was dead quiet, and it smelled very old.

"We should have brought the flashlight," Stephanie said as she stepped through the door. "I can't see a thing."

Rebecca and I didn't speak. I was counting, and I think she was, too. Two minutes, Stephanie had said in her dare. One, one thousand; two, one thousand; three, one thousand. . . . I'd gotten to forty-two, one thousand when I heard the noise, kind of a clicking sound.

You're letting your imagination run away with you again, Lauren, I scolded myself.

But then Rebecca gasped — she must have heard it, too.

A few seconds later, Stephanie said, "Is one of you making that noise?"

"N-no . . . ," I stammered.

Rebecca didn't answer at all — she just grabbed onto my arm with both hands and squeezed.

It wasn't really a clicking sound, it was more of a . . . a . . . *tapping*! I swallowed hard. It was getting nearer . . . nearer. . . . Suddenly something knocked against the wall of the shed, JUST OUTSIDE THE DOOR!

Rebecca and I both screamed at the top of our lungs!

Stephanie squared her shoulders, stuck her head out the door, and burst out laughing! "It's Sleepover," she announced. "The escape artist strikes again."

"Sleepover." I let my breath out with a *whooosh*! I felt as though I'd been holding it for about five minutes.

"Do you think anybody heard us scream?" Rebecca said as we scrambled out of the dreaded shed.

She stared down the hill at the four houses on the Newman farm, but the only lights we could see were the sleepover lights: the ones on the third floor of her own house, where our bedrooms were, and the ones on the bottom floor, where the other girls were waiting. We hadn't woken anybody up.

"The shed must have muffled the noise," Rebecca said.

"Yeah — they just don't make 'em like they used to," I mumbled.

Stephanie was hanging on to Sleepover's halter, giggling. "The two of you screamed loud enough to knock the shed down, like the Big Bad Wolf."

But I didn't like the giggling. "Admit it, Stephanie," I said. "You were scared, too — maybe just for a second, but definitely scared. You asked us if we were making the noise. . . ," I reminded her.

"I was just trying to figure out what direction it was coming from," Stephanie said huffily. "No way do I believe in ghosts." She giggled again. "It was just poor old Sleepover, following us up here and clinking his halter."

"How did he get out?" Rebecca wondered, turning her attention to the burro. "Somebody must have left his stall door open. . . ."

"Uh-uh," I said. "The door was closed when we visited him tonight. Reggie checked the latch before we left."

"First he finessed the ropes, and now latches," said Stephanie. "Sleepover is really talented."

"Let's get him back down to the barn," Rebecca said. "We'll have to try to find a lock for his stall like the one your father had on the trailor, Stephanie."

We started back down the hill, with Stephanie giggling every few steps. "You should have heard yourselves," she'd say, and crack up. Or, "Ghosts! Really, guys."

I was about ready to throttle her when we cut through the row of birch trees and Stephanie stopped cold. Sleepover's head rose and he pricked up his ears.

"Look!" Stephanie said so softly that I could barely hear her. "Sleepover sees them, too — right over there, near the fence. They're coming toward us. . . ." Her voice cracked.

"What?" Rebecca and I whispered.

"WOLVES!" Stephanie absolutely screeched. She turned Sleepover loose and ran, faster than I've ever seen her run, down the hill toward Rebecca's grandparents' house.

Lights were blinking on in the bedrooms in all four of the houses, and the "wolves" started to bark — George and Martha, Rebecca's collies, out for an evening stroll.

"*Wolves!*" Rebecca chortled.

"Stephanie is basically a city kid," I said, giggling. "And she'd just mentioned the Big Bad Wolf — I guess it stuck in her mind." Stephanie's imagination had acted up as much as ours had — it just took something other than ghosts to set if off.

"Oh, no," Rebecca said suddenly. "Not *that* way!" she yelled at Stephanie's retreating back, since there was no reason to be quiet now.

But it was too late. We heard a splash. . . .

Rebecca and I looked at each other and cracked up. "The pond!"

Chapter
8

I think Stephanie woke up everybody on the farm, including Sally, the baby, with her yelling. Still, the Newmans were nice about it, even though they would be waking up again in about four hours.

Stephanie stood on Rebecca's back porch, dripping wet, her teeth chattering. Uncle Jeff had pulled her out of the pond.

"Rebecca, let your father take the donkey back to the barn. And you look for some big towels for Stephanie, all right?" Mrs. Newman directed.

We went to bed soon after that. I noticed there wasn't much talk about how dumb it is to be scared of ghosts . . . or *wolves*.

I'd planned to jog early Sunday morning. Instead, Reggie's mom invited us all to a pancake feast, with quarts of syrup from their own maple trees.

Then Mr. Jones came for Molly and Patti in his black Jeep. Annette's mom picked her and Stephanie up, and Darlene caught a ride home with them. Just Kate and I were left at Rebecca's.

We learned from Rebecca's dad how to hook up a cow to a milking machine. We helped Reggie feed the calves their snack of watered-down milk. And we turned Sleepover out into the fenced-in pasture behind the houses.

Right away, he started to plod up and down the fence, kind of pushing at it with his nose.

"He's trying to escape again," Kate said.

"He won't be able to this time," said Grandpa Newman, who was watching Sleepover with us. "That's a strong fence — built it myself years ago."

"There's plenty of space in this pasture for him to run and play and get all the exercise he needs," I said. "Why does he want out? Where does he want to go?"

"Back to Arizona, maybe. Maybe after the wide, open spaces, all of this looks too tame," Grandpa Newman said with a smile.

Was that it? Was Sleepover *bored*?

We had lunch at Uncle Jeff's and Aunt Maureen's house — "It won't be much," she'd said, and then went on to stuff us with chicken lasagna and hot apple pie.

Reggie and his dad left in their truck after lunch to meet the Riverhurst bus. Mark Freedman would be Reggie's guest for the week, which I knew meant nonstop baseball. Mark lives and breathes baseball.

Sure enough, they'd barely gotten back from Walden, and Reggie and Mark and Reggie's little brother, David, were outside next to the barn, taking turns at bat.

We were sprawled on Rebecca's front porch in the shade, too full to even talk.

"Come on, girls — help us out!" Reggie said.

"Yeah — if even two of you'd play, we could have a good game of catch-up," Mark wheedled.

"Go away," Kate said firmly.

"We're digesting our food," Rebecca added.

I just groaned, softly.

"Hey — here come the Barneses!" Reggie said, looking toward the highway.

Kate shaded her eyes and squinted at the green station wagon as it sped up the gravel lane. "It's them, all right," she said with a sigh. "I'll get my suitcase."

When Kate squeezed into the Barneses' station wagon, she looked about as happy as she'd probably look on her way to jail.

"Good-bye!" Mr. Barnes boomed cheerfully. But Kate didn't even wave as they roared away down the gravel drive.

"I feel terrible for her," I said.

"Maybe the kids were especially wild yesterday because they'd been cooped up in their grandmother's house," Rebecca said. "Maybe when they get home and work off some steam, they'll act like human beings."

"You really think so?" I asked her.

Rebecca gazed after the car for a few seconds before shaking her head. "Probably not," she admitted.

And the next morning, when Reggie, Mark, Rebecca, and I, and the little Newmans and Bennetts got on the school bus, I could tell from Kate's face that it hadn't happened.

Will and the twins were the first kids we saw, because they were sitting up front, right next to the bus driver. The three of them wiggled their fingers at us and smiled like perfect angels.

"They seem a lot quieter," I murmured to Rebecca as we started down the aisle. "Do you think

Kate got them under control somehow?"

"Uh-uh," said Rebecca. "It's Mrs. Croker, the bus driver." She was a large person, dressed in a navy pantsuit and wearing a cap. "She's one tough woman, and she always makes them sit where she can keep an eye on them."

We'd hardly taken three steps when Mrs. Croker barked from behind us, "Will Barnes! Hand over that squirt gun, or I'll personally hogtie you and drag you into Principal Dahlen's office!"

"I see what you mean," I said to Rebecca.

"Hey, guys — hi, Lauren." It was Pete Stone, sitting with Austin Albers. Pete has wavy brown hair and green eyes, and he's taller than I am, which isn't that usual among Riverhurst fifth-graders. He had on a really cool-looking striped sweatshirt that I've seen him wear to parties. "Lauren, you missed a great bus ride up here yesterday," Pete went on.

Angela Kemp was sitting right behind him, her beady brown eyes locked on me. So I just smiled at Pete and nodded. There was no way Angela was going to be report to Jenny Carlin that I'd been chasing after Pete!

Carol Harrison was sitting next to Angela, and she gave Rebecca and me a friendly grin. She knew all about my problems with Jenny and Angela, from her trip to Riverhurst. "Hi, Lauren," Carol said. "It's nice to see you in Walden."

"Thanks, Carol," I said.

I glanced over at Angela and couldn't believe my eyes! Was I imagining things, or was that a friendly smile creeping across Angela's thin lips?

"Want to sit with us?" Carol asked.

"No thanks — Kate's in the back," Rebecca said. *"Did you see that?"* she whispered after we'd moved up the aisle. "I think Angela smiled at us!"

"Maybe Carol's a good influence," I said. Jenny Carlin would die if she knew!

Wanda and Kate were undoubtedly trying to put as much space as possible between themselves and the three younger Barneses. If they'd been any farther away from Will and the twins, they'd have been sitting outside the bus.

I plopped down beside Kate on the long seat running across the back of the bus. "How's it going?" I whispered.

"Not good," Kate murmured. "Tell you later."

The bus made a few more stops and then rolled into town. Mrs. Croker pulled up right next to the front sidewalk of the elementary school and opened the bus doors.

"End of the line!" she said. "Everybody out. Walk, don't run."

"My water gun, Mrs. Croker?" I heard Will Barnes whine.

"You can have it this afternoon — when I let you out at your house!" Mrs. Croker thundered. "And not a second before!"

Stephanie and Annette and Patti and Molly were waiting for us near the front steps. Molly and Wanda started talking about a Walden Elementary School band concert — they both play clarinet. That gave Kate a chance to tell the rest of us about the Barneses.

"Mr. Barnes is nice," Kate said in a low voice, "but he's in a different world, with his sheep."

"Sheep?" Stephanie repeated.

"Leicester sheep," Kate said. "He's one of the biggest breeders of Leicester sheep in the state. When he's not busy with his sheep in the barn or in the pasture, he's thinking about them. What he doesn't notice doesn't bother him, and if it isn't sheep, he doesn't notice. Will and the twins get away with *murder*."

"What about Frank?" I asked. "Won't he help with the kids?"

"Frank thinks he's too grown-up and too cool

to pay any attention to the younger kids, as long as they stay out of his way. He lifts weights, plays his tape deck, talks to his girlfriend on the phone . . . you know," Kate replied.

"And Wanda?" Patti said.

"Wanda." Kate frowned. "She's too nice — they run all over her, and she just tries to repair the damage."

"Sort of a wimp," Stephanie said. "In other words."

Kate nodded, looking discouraged.

"Have you tried being firm?" Patti asked her. "And keeping them busy?"

Kate sighed. "There's plenty for them to do — they just won't do it. Their rooms are a total mess, but they won't even make up the beds. If I say anything, they just laugh and run out of the house."

"Does Wanda do anything about it?" I asked.

"I've tried to toughen her up, but she just says, 'Oh, that's how little kids are,' " Kate replied. "She clears the table for them, does all the dishes, even straightens up their rooms."

"Little kids? Will is *eight*," Annette pointed out.

"Yeah, and he's the worst. Mandy and Thomas copy him," Kate said.

"Hmm . . ." said Stephanie, looking thoughtful.

"Maybe I should give you a hand — "

"A sense of humor is *not* going to make a dif-ference," Kate interrupted. "And they think of *fun* things to do all on their own — like wrecking the place!"

"I'm sure I could — "

"When I need help, I'll ask for it!" Kate growled at her. "What you know about kids, Stephanie, could fit on the head of a pin!"

"You want to bet?" Stephanie said heatedly.

"Come on, guys," Patti said, trying to shush them before Wanda overheard.

Luckily, the first bell rang before Kate and Stephanie could really get going. We filed into the building along with Molly, Wanda, and everyone else.

"How's Sleepover doing?" Stephanie asked me as we followed the Walden girls into 5A, Ms. Pow-ell's fifth-grade class.

"No more escapes," I reported. "But he's still not eating much, except for the junk the little kids feed him." I didn't tell her, but I thought Rebecca's dad and Grandpa Newman were kind of worried about him.

We all found seats — enough desks had been shoved into the room for the Riverhurst kids. Ms.

77

Powell, our teacher for the week, was pleasant-looking, with dark skin and short brown hair. As soon as everybody was settled, Ms. Powell said, "Let's give our guests a big Walden welcome!"

All the Walden kids clapped and even whistled.

But we found out right away that we weren't on vacation, because the next thing she said was, "Take out your math workbooks, class, and turn to page forty-nine. I've made copies for the visitors. . . ."

Chapter
9

After lunch in the Walden cafeteria, Stephanie, Patti, and I tracked down Tommy Nixon. He's a thin boy who, if he ever grows into his hands and feet, should make a great basketball player.

In fact, we found him on the outdoor basketball court with Pete and Mark and Larry from our class, and Reggie and some of the other guys. Tommy had stayed with Pete in Riverhurst, and Larry was his visitor now. The reason we wanted to talk to Tommy, though, is that his father is a veterinarian, and Tommy's had a lot of experience with animals himself.

We told Tommy about Sleepover, from the time he arrived in Stephanie's driveway, to this morning, when he wouldn't touch his oats.

"Well . . . it sounds to me like he's bored," Tommy said.

Bored? That's exactly what I'd been thinking! "But he seemed okay in the beginning, when he was at Happy Trails," Stephanie pointed out.

"Until he got used to things," Tommy said. "Like stables and trailers and Shetland ponies and stuff. As soon as they were old news, he got bored."

"And in Arizona, he was free to roam as far as he liked . . . ," Patti said.

"Right — plenty of different scenery, lots of new burros to get to know, antelopes to look at, and probably even buffalo . . . ," Tommy said.

If he was right, Sleepover would never be happy in Riverhurst, *or* on the farm — in fact, he would never be happy staying in one place. That was a very sad thought.

That afternoon, while we were getting on the bus, Angela Kemp actually started talking to me! "Hi, Lauren," she said, "Hasn't this trip been fun so far?"

I was so shocked that all I could mumble was, "Oh — sure — yeah — definitely."

Rebecca and I sat at the back with Kate and Wanda again. Kate had cheered up a little at school, since she didn't have Will and the twins to deal with.

But I knew she must be dreading going back to the Barneses'.

I waited until Reggie started talking to Wanda about Frank Barnes's next wrestling match. Then I whispered to Kate, "Why don't you spend the rest of the week at Rebecca's? There's plenty of room" — and more than enough food — "and I'm sure it'd be okay with the Newmans."

"I'd feel bad about running out on Wanda," Kate murmured. She takes her responsibilities seriously.

"Maybe when her mother gets back. . . ," I said.

"Nobody seems to know when *that* will be," Kate said.

"Then we'll just come over a lot." I turned to Rebecca, on my other side. "Do you think we could go over to the Barneses' this afternoon?" I asked her in a low voice. "Kate could use some support."

"Sure — we'll borrow Reggie's bike for you, since he and Mark will be playing baseball, anyway," Rebecca said.

Kate's face brightened a little. "Thanks, guys."

There were only a few stops before the bus got to the Newman farm. We were almost even with the white iron gate when Mrs. Croker screeched to a stop and practically sat on the horn.

"What is it?" "What's happening?" all the kids were yelling.

"It's a dumb *donkey*!" Will Barnes announced loudly from his seat in front. "Where does it think it's going?"

"Grandpa Newman says back to Arizona," David Bennett volunteered.

"It's Sleepover again!" Rebecca and I groaned.

He was walking right down the center stripe on the road, happy as a clam.

"See you later," we said hurriedly to Kate and Wanda.

Mrs. Croker opened the bus doors, and Rebecca and I jumped out, along with Reggie and Mark, David and Bess Bennett, and Rebecca's little sisters.

"I've got a candy bar," David said, digging it out of his pants pocket.

"Candy, Sleepover," Tracy called out as we trotted after the burro.

As soon as he heard us behind him, he stopped walking and waggled his long ears. He let Reggie grab his halter and lead him out of the road, so that Mrs. Croker could start the bus up again.

"Bad donkey," Janis scolded, while Sleepover munched on David's candy bar. "Do you want to get run over?"

And there came Grandpa Newman, huffing and puffing down the gravel lane. "Turns out he *could* get through that fence I made," Grandpa said when he reached us.

The Barneses' farm was only two miles down the road from the Newmans'. After Rebecca and I had had a snack — big bowls of the peach ice cream her mom had made — we biked over.

The sheep looked the way Patti had described them — grazing in the pasture, they were like fluffy clouds floating across a green sky. Leicester sheep are all white, with broad backs and very thick fleece that hangs down in loose curls.

"I wish my hair would do that," I said as we leaned our bikes against the Barneses' fence. My hair has always been one of my major trouble spots.

"I know what you mean," said Rebecca. Her hair's as straight as mine.

The Barneses live in a white two-story house with blue shutters. Rebecca knocked at the front door and waited . . . and waited.

"I'm sure they're in there," I said.

When no one came, Rebecca tried the knob. "It's not locked," she said, pushing the door open.

Right away it was clear why no one had heard

us: There was a lot of yelling going on.

"If you want to live like a pig, that's your business!" Wanda's voice. "Just don't wreck the rest of the house!"

"Well, at least Kate has toughened Wanda up," Rebecca murmured to me.

But it didn't seem to have done any good. Maybe Wanda didn't sound as though she meant it, because Will shrieked. "You're not my mom, and I don't have to listen to you! You'd better get off my case!" Will's voice was soon followed by Will himself, stamping down the stairs. "Out of my way!" he yelled at us, just before he dashed out the door.

"Kate? Wanda?" we called out.

"Up here," Kate answered. Her voice sounded muffled, as if she were far away.

We climbed the stairs. There was a piece of a train set on the third step. A book on the fifth. A shoe higher up. Rebecca and I exchanged glances.

The upstairs hall was a minor disaster area. More pieces of the train set, the other shoe, clothes, games; you name it and at least one piece of it was among the clutter.

"And I thought *I* was messy," I said to Rebecca as we picked our way down the hall. The mess was getting noticeably worse.

We stepped over a soccer ball, one rubber boot, and a jigsaw puzzle. I peeked inside a bedroom as we passed.

"This one's neat," I said.

"Mr. and Mrs. Barnes's?" Rebecca suggested.

"Probably."

"Look, so is this one, more or less," Rebecca said, peering into another bedroom.

"Gotta be Frank's," I said. "See the barbells? Oh, and look at that neat scale! Remind me to check it out — these farm meals aren't exactly slimming." The scale was one of those electronic ones.

As we clambered through the debris, the twins watched us silently — each one sucking on a finger — from the end of the hallway. They stood in front of a bedroom door that, judging from the pink curtains and guest cot, had to be Wanda's, and it was some mess!

"What happened in here?" Rebecca asked Wanda and Kate, who stood in the middle of the room.

"We told Will to clean his room," Wanda began.

"So he did," Kate went on, "by throwing all of his stuff into Wanda's room. Then he threw all of Wanda's and my things onto the floor, too!"

85

"Very nice," said Rebecca.

"We're just trying to hang on until Mrs. Barnes gets back," Kate said with a sigh. She pitched a shoe and sock into a growing pile in the hallway. "I think I'll have to give in — see if Stephanie can manage any better." Kate was going to ask Stephanie for help? She must have been totally discouraged.

The twins rushed downstairs to watch TV as soon as we started to straighten — they certainly weren't going to get caught doing housework.

Rebecca and I stayed until the four of us had cleared out the upstairs hall. Wanda was dragging out the vacuum cleaner when Rebecca said, "We'd better head for home. It's almost dinnertime."

Dinner! Mrs. Newman was going to make chicken and dumplings and chocolate meringue pie.

"Good luck with the monsters," I said to Kate.

"See you on the bus," she said. "If I'm still alive."

Rebecca and I were almost out the front door when Thomas appeared from the living room.

"Did you remember to weigh yourself?" he asked, smiling.

Rebecca and I had both forgotten about it. "Thanks, Thomas." I smiled back. "Maybe there's hope for the twins," I whispered to Rebecca. "I'll be down in a second."

Frank's scale is one of those that talks to you. But when I heard what it had to say, I almost flipped. "You weigh ninety-five pounds," it announced in a robot voice.

"Ninety-five pounds!" But I'd weighed only eighty-nine on Friday! I'd been on the scales at home because I was weighing my kitten, Rocky. I had gained *six* pounds in *three* days, and if I kept it up I was going to be the blimp I'd dreamed about!

I guess I looked kind of funny when I walked out of Frank's room, because Kate asked, "Is everything okay?"

"Oh, yeah," I mumbled. "It's fine — see you tomorrow."

Five more days of fabulous farm food, and I wasn't going to be able to eat any of it!

Chapter
10

The next morning I set my alarm for six o'clock, and jogged up and down the road for a couple of miles. After that I looked in on Sleepover. He yawned when he saw me, but I couldn't tell if he was bored, or if he was just sleepy.

For breakfast Mrs. Newman made blueberry muffins and sausages. It was agony, but all I ate was half a grapefruit.

"That wouldn't keep a bird alive," Mrs. Newman said.

I smiled bravely and thought of the blimp.

When we got on the school bus, Carol and Angela moved back to sit with Kate and Wanda and Rebecca and me.

"I'm planning a sleepover this Friday," Carol

told us. "All of you are invited, plus Patti and Molly and Annette and Stephanie and Darlene and Jane Sykes. There'll be lots of good stuff to eat — my mom and dad are both great cooks."

I groaned silently — more food I'd have to turn down.

"And my dad's going to get us tickets to the circus!" Carol went on.

"What circus?" Kate asked.

"Clive Barty's Traveling Tent Show!" Carol said.

"Oh — I saw the poster in Albright's window," I remembered.

"It comes to Walden for a few days every year," Wanda said.

"They have terrific animal acts, like trained ponies and elephants," said Carol, "and a man who can squeeze himself into a tiny glass box, and trapeze artists. . . ."

"Lauren and I will definitely be there," Rebecca said, and I nodded — I love circuses.

"We'll come, too," Kate said. "Right, Wanda?"

"Do you think Daddy and the kids can manage without us?" Wanda said worriedly.

"They'll *manage*." Kate was firm.

I sneaked a look at Angela. How would she feel

about a sleepover with her sworn enemies?

She was actually smiling! Had someone else — someone *nice* — gotten trapped in Angela Kemp's body?

The bus pulled up at Walden Elementary, and Kate rushed off to look for Stephanie. When we finally caught up with her, the two of them were deep in conversation near the swings.

"I don't know. . . ," Stephanie was saying. "You've been pretty rude about my child-managing ideas."

I remembered the "head of a pin" remark myself.

"Come on, Stephanie!" Kate pleaded. "I've tried hard with Will and the twins, but nothing seems to work, and they're driving us crazy!"

"Well. . . ," Stephanie said slowly.

"If you can make them behave, I'll . . . I'll never argue with you again!" Kate promised. She was really desperate.

Stephanie grinned at Rebecca and me. "I'll do it then, as soon as Annette's mom has the time to drive us over."

"This afternoon after school, I'm pretty sure," Annette said.

"So it's settled," said Kate. For once, she really wanted Stephanie to prove her wrong.

Rebecca and I didn't go to the Barneses' house that afternoon, because Mr. Newman wanted to take us to a cattle auction. It was kind of neat — the auctioneer talked so fast that I couldn't understand a word, but the other people did, raising their fingers now and then to bid on a cow or calf. Mr. Newman bought a young cow, and we brought her home in the back of his pickup.

Rebecca and I had just walked into the kitchen when the telephone rang. Rebecca picked it up. It was Kate.

"Hi, Kate. Did Stephanie come?"

Rebecca held the phone so that I could hear Kate, too.

"Yes," Kate said, sounding excited.

"And?" said Rebecca.

"I don't know what she did," said Kate. "But there's been a complete change around here!"

"What do you mean?" I asked her.

"Stephanie wanted to be alone with Will and the twins, so the four of them went into Will's room and closed the door," Kate reported. "When the door opened again, everybody was smiling. Will and

91

Thomas and Mandy started cleaning up their rooms right away, and now they're in the basement, doing the laundry!"

"You're kidding!" Rebecca and I exclaimed. A good sense of humor would do all that? Maybe she'd treated Will like an artist. Or had Stephanie somehow convinced the three of them that cleaning and washing were *fun* things?

"Gotta go," Kate said. "Mandy wants to help me set the table for dinner."

"Let's call Stephanie!" I said as soon as Kate had hung up.

But nobody answered at the Hollises'. "They must have gone out to eat," Rebecca said. We'd have to wait till the next day to get the details.

Speaking of eating, I wasn't doing any. It killed me, but that night at dinner all I had was some salad and one pork chop. No potatoes, no cornbread, no cake.

Things improved the next morning, though. I'd just started jogging down the gravel lane when Reggie caught up with me. He was wearing sweatpants and running shoes, too. "Hi," he said. "Mind. if I join you?"

"Where's Mark?" I asked him.

Reggie laughed. "Still sleeping — he hates getting up early."

Jogging alone is okay. Jogging with my brother Roger is nicer. Jogging with Reggie Bennett is . . . excellent!

When Rebecca and I got on the school bus that day, I was half expecting Kate to tell us that things had fallen apart at the Barneses'.

"Everything's fine," Kate said when we asked her. "The kids were perfect. Will even vacuumed the downstairs this morning."

I couldn't believe it! He didn't get into trouble with Mrs. Croker *once* during the bus ride, either. We were dying to know how Stephanie had done it.

But she wouldn't tell us! She just smiled mysteriously and said, "You all hooted at my ideas. Why should I give away the secrets of my success?"

Patti and I did notice Stephanie having a private conference under the swings with Will and the twins after lunch, but she shut up as soon as we got near them.

The Newmans' bathroom scale was broken, so I couldn't tell if my dieting and jogging were working. But Thursday morning, Reggie and I had just reached the road when Pete Stone and Austin Albers trotted over the hill!

"Hi, Lauren — Reggie," they said.

"This was a great idea," Pete added.

If Jenny Carlin could see me now, I thought, picking up some speed. I'm not chasing boys, they're chasing me!

Grandpa Newman had figured out a way to keep Sleepover from escaping from the pasture. First he'd repaired the fence. Then he'd taken a very long length of chain and hooked one end to Sleepover's halter. The other end he attached to a metal stake he'd pounded into the ground. Sleepover could graze in an enormous circle, but if he tried to run away, he'd have a chain and a fence to deal with. There was still the problem of Sleepover not being happy, though.

Tommy Nixon talked to Stephanie and me about it at lunch that day. "My dad said pretty much the same thing," Tommy told us. "The burro's bored."

"So what can we do about it?" Stephanie asked.

"My dad said you should try to keep him busy," Tommy replied.

"It sounds like Kate's child-managing ideas," Stephanie said with a grin.

"Maybe we should try *yours* on Sleepover," I suggested.

Stephanie shook her head. "They don't work on a donkey."

Chapter
11

Thursday afternoon, Rebecca and I stayed in Walden after school. Along with Annette and Stephanie, Patti and Molly, and Darlene and Jane Sykes, we went to the Doughnut Hole. Everybody else chose great, gooey jelly doughnuts, and I had a Diet Dr Pepper.

"Why aren't you eating anything, Lauren?" Stephanie asked.

"I'm not hungry," I growled.

Then we went to the Star Confectionery. Everybody else had the specialty, a hot butterscotch sundae. I had a lemon yogurt.

We stopped in at Albright's General Store, and looked at butter churns and hip boots and birdhouses. I bought my mom a cherry pitter. Stephanie bought a red T-shirt that said "Albright's Has It!" Patti bought a paperback book called *Reptiles of the U.S.* for her little brother, Horace, who's crazy about lizards and turtles and other creepy-crawlies.

Mrs. Newman picked Rebecca and me up in front of Albright's at four-thirty. We called Kate and Wanda as soon as we got home.

"Nothing new to report," Kate told us. "Everything's still going smoothly. I really have to hand it to Stephanie. She'll have her kid brother or sister trained in no time."

I jogged again with the guys on Friday morning. It would be our last run together, because I'd be at Carol's house on Saturday morning, and our bus would be leaving for Riverhurst on Saturday afternoon.

"I'll miss having somebody to jog with," Reggie said as we huffed up the hill.

"So will I," said Pete. "Maybe we can work something out in Riverhurst, though. . . ." he added to me.

Jenny Carlin would die!

I could see trouble as soon as the bus pulled up to the Newman farm. The Barnes kids always sit in the front seat near Mrs. Croker, and Mandy always sits next to the window. I nudged Rebecca, "Would you look at that?"

Mandy was wearing a black-and-white sweat-shirt. It was about two sizes too big for her . . . and it looked awfully familiar!

"Stephanie's sweatshirt!" Rebecca said, her eyes widening as she caught on.

"Right," I said. "She's been *bribing* them to be good!"

We jumped on the bus and rushed to the back seat. "What are you going to do?" Rebecca said to Kate and Wanda.

"About what?" Kate asked casually.

"Stephanie buying them off!" I said, pointing toward Will and the twins.

"We hadn't noticed," Kate said with a grin. "As long as it works. . . ."

"I can't tell you how peaceful it's been," Wanda added, gazing dreamily out the window.

So nobody said anything about the bribes to Stephanie. As long as it worked. . . .

Trouble was coming, though. After lunch, Rebecca spotted Stephanie and Will arguing on the side steps of the school. And we'd only been home about half an hour that afternoon when Kate called. We thought it was about their ride to Carol's house: Kate and Wanda were supposed to go with Rebecca and me in Mrs. Newman's car.

But the first thing Kate said was, "Will has disappeared!"

"He's probably out in the barn with Mr. Barnes or something," Rebecca told her.

"No — Mr. Barnes isn't back from Walden," Kate said grimly. "Frank's still at the high school, and the twins say they don't know anything."

"Is his bike there?" Rebecca asked.

"It is, but we've looked everywhere — Wanda thought he might have walked over to your place to play with David."

"David and Reggie and Mark went with Uncle Jeff to Hamilton for a tractor part," Rebecca told her.

"Then we'll look here again," Kate said.

"We'll come over and help you," Rebecca told her.

The four of us searched every inch of the Barnes farm, and all we saw were curly sheep.

Wanda was practically wringing her hands by the time we gave up and went back to the house. "I don't know what to do now," she said tearfully. "Should I call around Walden and try to reach Dad? Should I call Mom in Hamilton?"

Suddenly the phone rang. "If it's Will, I'll throttle him!" Kate said, grabbing it.

We all leaned closer to listen.

"This is Clive Barty of the Clive Barty Traveling Tent Show," a man's voice announced. "Are you missing a kid named Will?"

"He's at the circus!" Wanda sobbed.

"Yes, we are," said Kate. She looked mad enough to spit.

"Well, I've got him here with me. He says he wants to join the circus," said Mr. Barty, "but he looks a little young, so if you want to pick him up, he's in my trailer."

"Mom'll take us," Rebecca told Kate.

"We'll be right over," Kate said.

"I have something else I'd like to talk to you about," said Mr. Barty. "There's a good-looking donkey here that I understand belongs to one of you. . . ."

Houdini *would* have been a better name.

We all filed into the circus tent that evening: Carol, Angela, Darlene, Jane, Molly, Patti, Annette, Stephanie, Kate, Wanda, Rebecca, and me.

Angela was laughing and talking a mile a minute to Stephanie and Patti.

"How long do you think Angela's personality transplant will last?" I murmured to Kate.

"Until the second we step onto the Riverhurst bus," Kate predicted. "I just hope Wanda's is permanent."

That afternoon we'd seen a new Wanda. She was so upset when we finally caught up with Will in Mr. Barty's trailer that she'd boomed almost as loudly as her dad — and Will was so surprised that *he* apologized, for a change!

Mr. Harrison had gotten us a big box on the center ring, and the twelve of us just about filled it up.

"Isn't it neat?" Carol said, pointing to the tent overhead.

"I like the colors," said Stephanie. The canvas was printed with red and white stars and stripes.

"Speaking of colors, does Mandy get to keep your sweatshirt, Stephanie?" Rebecca asked.

"A deal is a deal. The twins were good — they get to keep whatever little things I gave them," Stephanie said.

"Peanuts! Popcorn!" a vendor yelled, and Carol beckoned him toward us.

"Who wants what?" she asked. "Dad gave me money for refreshments."

"No, thanks," I said when she got to me. Then I finally admitted it: "I was eating so much that when I hopped on Frank Barnes' scale, it said I'd put on six pounds!"

Wanda started to giggle. "Oh, no, Lauren," she said, "I'll bet you haven't. Thomas loves to fiddle with that scale!"

"Thomas!" I couldn't believe it! He had reminded me to weigh myself, but I never thought . . . "I'll have one giant bag of each," I told Carol, "and an extra-large Dr Pepper." All the fabulous farm meals I'd turned down! Still, those early-morning jogs weren't a total loss. . . .

"What about Will?" Molly was saying to Stephanie.

"He was too expensive," she replied. "He wanted the canoe in Albright's window, so he could paddle to the North Pole."

"That's the thing about bribes, Stephanie," Kate said. "Sooner or later, *nobody* can afford them."

"If Will hadn't gotten mad at me and tried to join the circus," Stephanie replied huffily, "we never would have met Clive Barty."

The circus band struck a chord. The lights flickered and went out. A spotlight shone on the ringmaster, dressed in a red jacket, white pants, and black boots. "Ladies and gentlemen, welcome to the three thousand two hundred and seventh performance of the wonderful Clive Barty Traveling Tent Show!"

As the performers rode into the tent on glossy white horses and enormous gray elephants, I leaned over to whisper in Kate's ear, "Donald Foster was right, in a way. One of us did join a traveling circus."

There, between a monkey riding a zebra and four little dogs dressed like ballerinas, was Sleepover. He was wearing a shiny red halter, and being led by a very spiffy clown.

"Well, he'll definitely have plenty of new places and things to look at," Kate said.

Sleepover waggled his ears happily and gave a great hee-haw!

SLEEPOVER
FRIENDS

#13 Patti's Secret Wish

"Just in time," said Stephanie. "There's Patti, coming around the park."

"I *knew* she wasn't baby-sitting for Horace," said Kate.

"She's going to be facing this way," I warned.

"Quick — grab a book!" Kate said.

We snatched some books from a pile in the window and held them up in front of our faces, in case Patti's gaze fell on the Bookloft. The three of us lowered our books just far enough so we could peer over them.

Patti locked her bike to the same bench as before. Then she took out a comb and began combing her hair.

"Good grief," Kate said. "Would you look at that!"

"Well, now we know exactly how bad things are," Kate said.

"I'm afraid it's even worse than that," Stephanie said suddenly. "Look at who's following *Patti* around."

Pack your bags for fun and adventure with

SLEEPOVER FRIENDS™
by Susan Saunders

Join Kate, Lauren, Stephanie and Patti at their great sleepover parties every weekend. Truth or Dare, scary movies, late-night boy talk—it's all part of **Sleepover Friends!**

America's Favorite Series

THE BABY-SITTERS CLUB®

by Ann M. Martin

Collect Them All!

The six girls at Stoneybrook Middle School get into all kinds of adventures...with school, boys, and, of course, baby-sitting!

☐ MG41124-1	**#10 Logan Likes Mary Anne!**	**$2.75**
☐ MG41125-X	**#11 Kristy and the Snobs**	**$2.75**
☐ MG41126-8	**#12 Claudia and the New Girl**	**$2.75**
☐ MG41127-6	**#13 Good-bye Stacey, Good-bye**	**$2.75**
☐ MG41128-4	**#14 Hello, Mallory**	**$2.75**
☐ MG41588-3	**Baby-sitters on Board! Special Edition #1**	**$2.95**
☐ MG41587-5	**#15 Little Miss Stoneybrook and Dawn**	**$2.75**
☐ MG41586-7	**#16 Jessi's Secret Language**	**$2.75**
☐ MG41585-9	**#17 Mary Anne's Bad Luck Mystery**	**$2.75**
☐ MG41584-0	**#18 Stacey's Mistake**	**$2.75**
☐ MG41583-2	**#19 Claudia and the Bad Joke**	**$2.75**
☐ MG42004-6	**#20 Kristy and the Walking Disaster**	**$2.75**
☐ MG42005-4	**#21 Mallory and the Trouble with Twins**	**$2.75**
☐ MG42006-2	**#22 Jessi Ramsey: Pet-Sitter**	**$2.75**
☐ MG42007-0	**#23 Dawn on the Coast**	**$2.75**
☐ MG42002-X	**#24 Kristy and the Mother's Day Surprise**	**$2.75**
☐ MG42003-8	**#25 Mary Anne and the Search for Tigger** (June '89)	**$2.75**
☐ MG42419-X	**Baby-sitters Summer Vacation Special Edition #2** (July '89)	**$2.95**
☐ MG42503-X	**#26 Claudia and Mimi** (August '89)	**$2.75**

PREFIX CODE 0-590-

Available wherever you buy books...or use the coupon below.

Scholastic Inc. P.O. Box 7502, 2932 E. McCarty Street, Jefferson City, MO 65102

Please send me the books I have checked above. I am enclosing $_____
(please add $1.00 to cover shipping and handling). Send check or money order–no cash or C.O.D.'s please.

Name_____

Address_____

City_____ State/Zip_____

Please allow four to six weeks for delivery. Offer good in U.S.A. only. Sorry, mail order not available to residents of Canada.   Prices subject to change.   BSC1288